LOST ON EARTH

BY JEFF DINARDO
ILLUSTRATED BY DAVE CLEGG

Funny Bone Books
and Funny Bone Readers are produced and published by
Red Chair Press LLC PO Box 333 South Egremont, MA 01258-0333
www.redchairpress.com

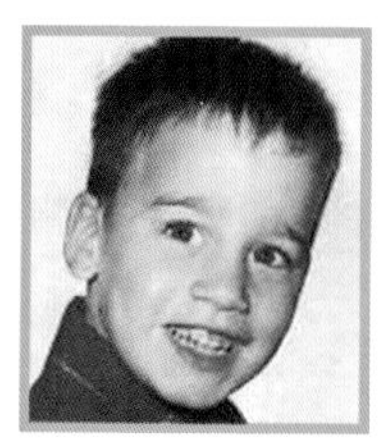

About the Author

Jeff Dinardo's books are filled with humor and silliness that captures a child's imagination. When not writing, Jeff runs a successful design firm specializing in textbooks for use in classrooms from K-8.

About the Artist

Dave Clegg lives and works on a small horse farm in north Georgia with his wife Lyn. All of Dave's work is done digitally on his computer. When he is not drawing, he can be found creating songs with his guitar or making robot sculptures!

Publisher's Cataloging-In-Publication Data
Names: Dinardo, Jeffrey. | Clegg, Dave, illustrator.
Title: The Jupiter twins. Book 2, Lost on Earth / by Jeff Dinardo ; illustrated by Dave Clegg.
Other Titles: Lost on Earth

Description: South Egremont, MA : Red Chair Press, [2018] | Series: Funny bone books. First chapters | Interest age level: 005-007. | Summary: "Trudy and Tina are best friends. They are also twins. Trudy loves adventure and Tina is happy to go along for the ride--as long as it is a smooth ride! Today the class is heading home from a field trip when the Space Bus has a problem. The teacher must make a landing on the mysterious planet Earth. First Chapters books are easy introductions to exploring longer text."--Provided by publisher.

Identifiers: LCCN 2017934023 | ISBN 978-1-63440-250-7 (library hardcover) | ISBN 978-1-63440-254-5 (paperback) | ISBN 978-1-63440-258-3 (ebook)

Subjects: LCSH: Twins--Juvenile fiction. | Earth (Planet)--Juvenile fiction. | Outer space--Exploration--Juvenile fiction. | School field trips--Juvenile fiction. | CYAC: Twins--Fiction. | Earth (Planet)--Fiction. | Outer space--Exploration--Fiction. | School field trips--Fiction.

Classification: LCC PZ7.D6115 Jul 2018 (print) | LCC PZ7.D6115 (ebook) | DDC [E]--dc23

Printed in Canada

0118 2P FRNS18

Contents

MEET THE CHARACTERS

TRUDY

TINA

MS. BICKLEBLORB

RIBBIT

QUACK

1 A QUIET RIDE

The space bus was quietly rumbling through space on its way back to Jupiter. The gentle rocking of the engines was so soothing that most of the kids had fallen asleep.

The twins Trudy and Tina were wide awake. They were busy playing a game of Tic Tac Toe to pass the time.

"You win again," said Tina.

Trudy was the school's Tic Tac Toe champion and she seldom lost.

Ms. Bickleblorb, their teacher, was behind the wheel. They were just coming back from a tour of the Milky Way and it had been a perfect field trip.

2 WATCH OUT!

A strange formation was in the distance.

It was a meteor shower.

Trudy and Tina saw it heading right for them.

"WATCH OUT!" they yelled.

Ms. Bickleblorb swerved at the last second.

THUMP.

One small meteor had hit the right rocket booster.

"Rats," said Ms. Bickleblorb. "We better land someplace so I can look at the damage."

She looked out the space bus window and saw a blue and green planet below.

"We can land there," she said.

Tina nudged her sister. "What planet is that?" she asked.

Trudy pulled out her textbook and looked it up.

"It's an unexplored, wild planet," she said. "It's called Earth."

Ms. Bickleblorb gently eased the space bus down in an open field on the planet's surface.

Everyone hopped out to inspect the damage.

"It's very hot here," said Tina.

"We are much closer to the sun than at home," said Ms. Bickleblorb. "It's not too bad," she added. "I can get this fixed in a jiffy."

Ms. Bickleblorb pulled out her tool box and got to work.

All the kids climbed back on the bus except the twins. Trudy was looking off into the distance. Tina knew her sister was up to no good.

"What are you doing?" she said. "This is an unexplored planet!"

"Not for long," said Trudy. "Come on."

3 A NEW WORLD

Tina and Trudy wandered over high hills and low valleys and made their way into a nearby forest.

"Look at these strange trees," said Tina.

"Everything is so colorful," said Trudy as she took out her notebook and started sketching.

While Trudy sketched and took notes, Tina smelled each kind of tree.

The sun was high overhead and it was still very hot.

Tina wiped the sweat from her face. "We should get back to the space bus."

Trudy put her notebook away and looked around. "There is one problem," she said. "We're lost."

“Lost!” yelled Tina. “But you always know where we are!”

Trudy shrugged. “We’ll just ask an Earthling how to get back. There must be some around here.”

Tina hopped up and down. “No, we can’t do that,” she said. “We don’t know what they are like. Maybe they are monsters. We should stay far away from them!”

“Too late,” laughed Trudy. “There is one right behind you.”

4 EARTHLINGS

"RIBBIT, RIBBIT," said the Earthling.

"Oh isn't he cute," said Trudy.

Tina bowed down. "We come in peace," she said.

"RIBBIT, RIBBIT," said the Earthling again and he hopped away.

"Let's follow him," said Trudy.

The Earthling hopped through the grass and plopped into a small pond.

SPLASH.

There were lots of other Earthlings already there.

“That looks fun,” said Trudy as she jumped into the cool water.

SPLASH.

Trudy and the Earthlings took turns jumping into the pond. They were all having fun.

"Come on in," Trudy said to Tina. "It's nice and cool in here!"

Tina wiped the sweat from her brow. "Maybe just once," Tina said, and she jumped in too.

SPLASH.

As the Jupiter twins played in the pond, more kinds of Earthlings joined in. Some had feathers, some had wings, but all were having fun.

"I guess all Earthlings are friendly," said Tina.

Just then, there was a loud snapping sound from the center of the pond.

SNAP, SNAP, SNAP.

The other Earthlings started to quickly hop, jump or fly out of the pond.

A huge scaly Earthling with a long snout and sharp teeth was trying to get them.

“*Jumping Jupiter!* This isn’t good,” yelled Trudy.

SNA

SNAP

5 Time to Go

Tina nearly fainted.

"Time to get out of here," said Trudy.

She ran over to the Earthling with feathers and told them they were lost.

"*QUACK, QUACK,*" was all the Earthling said, but she seemed to understand.

In a second, Tina and Trudy were flying in the sky, riding on the backs of two quacking Earthlings.

Tina held her eyes shut.

Trudy was enjoying the ride.

"There is the space bus!" she shouted.

The quacking Earthlings dropped off the twins next to the bus and flew away. Tina and Trudy watched them go.

“There you girls are!” said Ms. Bickleblorb. “The bus is all fixed and it’s time to go home.”

Once everyone was strapped in, the space bus raised up into the air.

Trudy opened her window.

"RIBBIT, RIBBIT, QUACK, QUACK," she shouted.

"What are you doing?" asked Tina.

"Just saying goodbye," said Trudy.

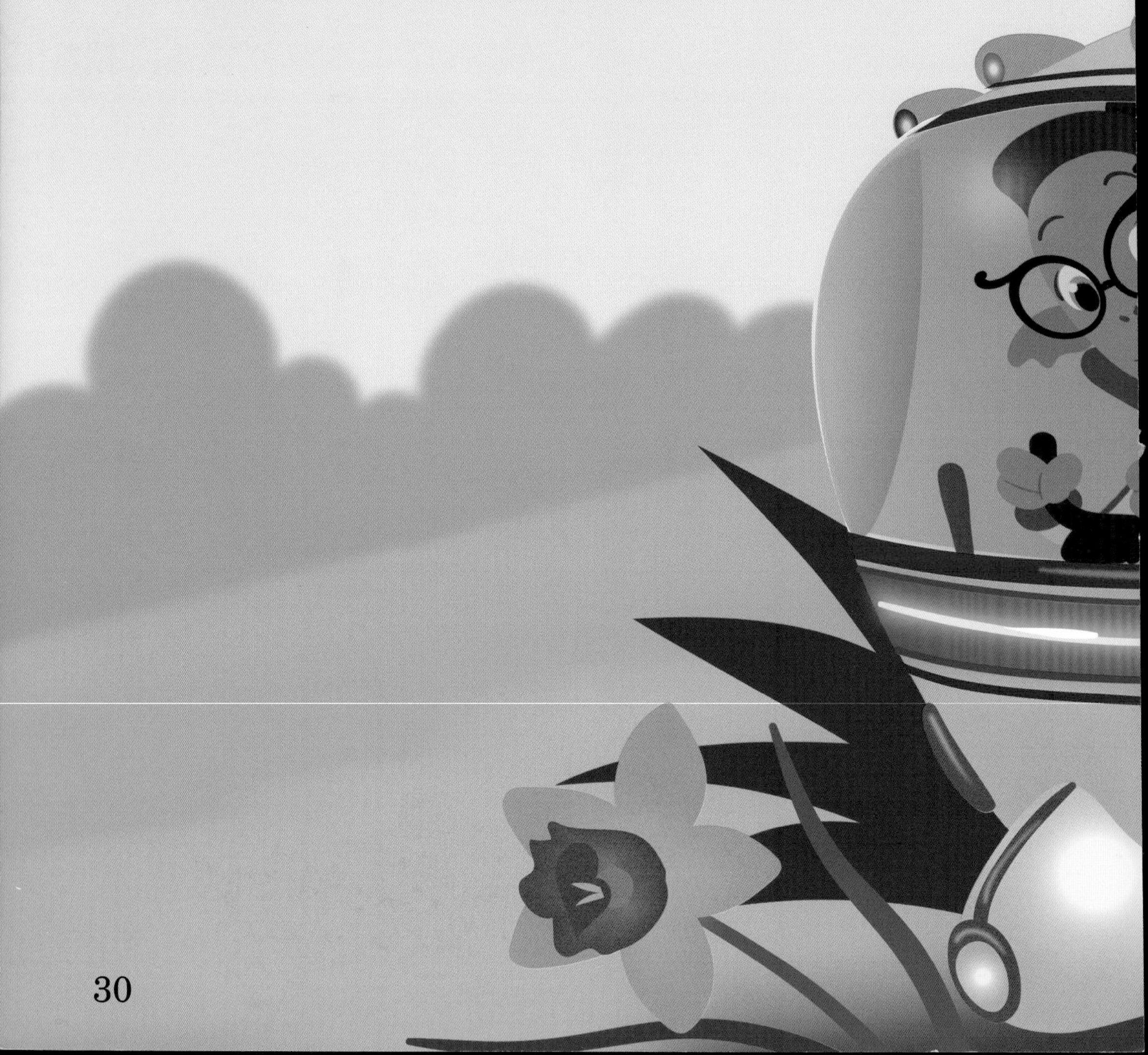

Tina opened her window.

"RIBBIT, RIBBIT, QUACK, QUACK," she shouted too.

"HONK, HONK, QUACK," replied the feathered Earthlings. Trudy was sure they said to come back again.